TEACHER!

Sharing, Helping, Caring

by **Patricia Hubbell**

illustrated by **Nancy Speir**

Marshall Cavendish Children

Marshall Cavendish Corporation, 99 White Plains Road, Tarrytown, NY 10591
www.marshallcavendish.us/kids

Library of Congress Cataloging-in-Publication Data

Hubbell, Patricia.
Teacher! : sharing, helping, caring / by Patricia Hubbell ; illustrated by Nancy Speir.
p. cm.
Summary: Illustrations and rhyming text depict a teacher helping students to learn and have fun during a week at school.
ISBN 978-0-7614-5574-5
[1. Stories in rhyme. 2. Schools—Fiction. 3. Teachers—Fiction.] I. Speir, Nancy, ill. II. Title.
PZ8.3.H848Te 2009
[E]—dc22
2008029403

The illustrations are rendered in acrylic paint on illustration board.
Book design by Anahid Hamparian
Editor: Margery Cuyler

Printed in Malaysia
First edition
1 3 5 6 4 2
mc Marshall Cavendish
Children

To my first-grade teacher, Mrs. Clevenger
—N.S.

Great big school! In we go!
Our teacher greets us, waves "hello!"

TODAY IS MONDAY

SPECIAL GUEST COMING SOON!

She helps us all to find our places—

finds our cubbies, ties our laces.

Gives us paper, crayons, glue.
Brings out paints—red, yellow, blue.

Shows us how to print our names,

sets out puzzles, blocks, and games.

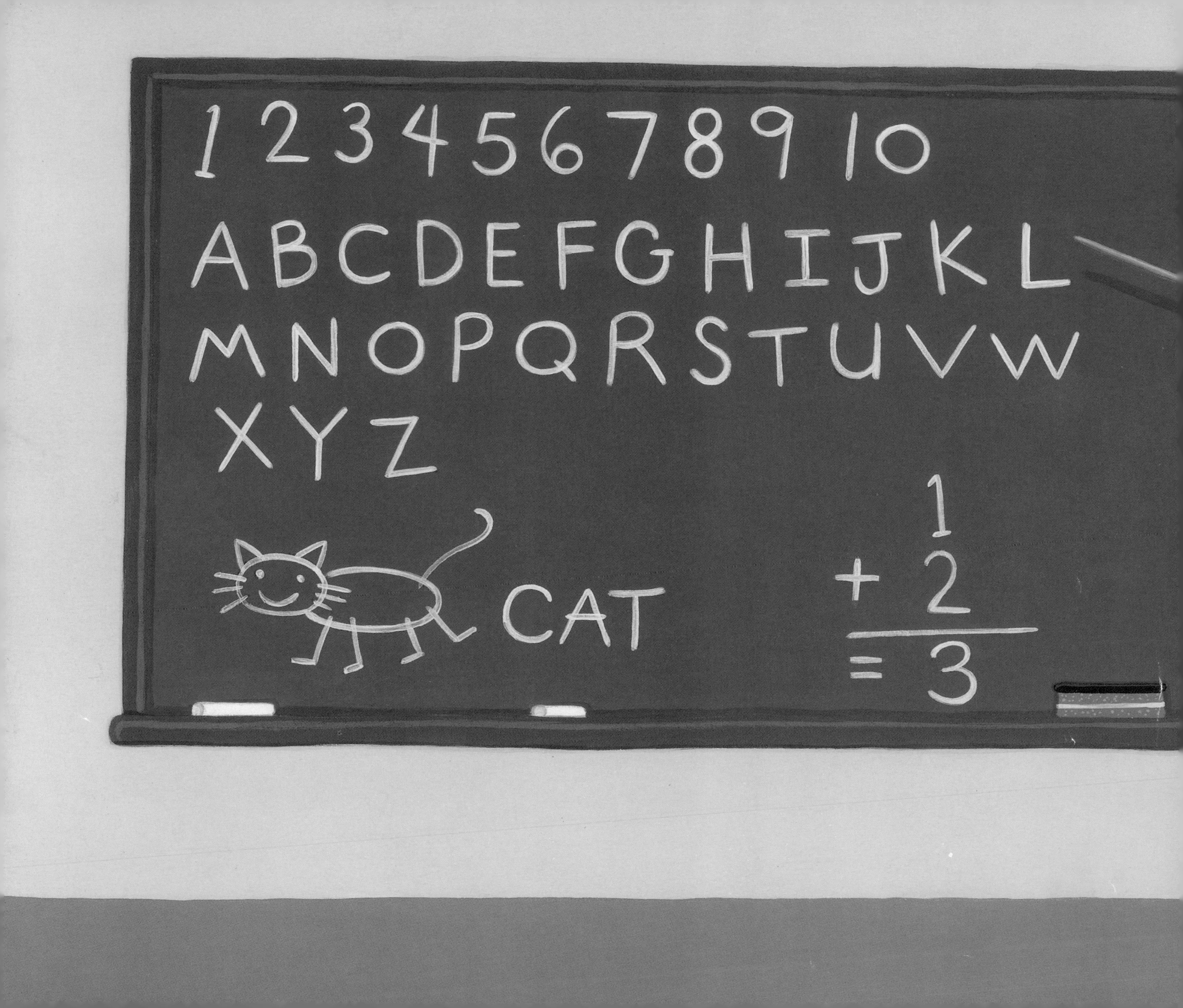

1 2 3 4 5 6 7 8 9 10

A B C D E F G H I J K L
M N O P Q R S T U V W
X Y Z

CAT

$$+\frac{1}{2} = 3$$

TODAY
IS
TUESDAY

SPECIAL
GUEST
COMING
SOON!

We learn our numbers, one, two, three,
and our letters, A, B, C.

We practice how to read and spell.
Teacher joins our show-and-tell.

She watches while we play outside.
We climb! We run! We crawl! We slide!

We all work in our garden plot . . .

plant pretty flowers in a pot.

Teacher helps us count out money,

lets us pet our classroom bunny.

TODAY IS WEDNESDAY

SPECIAL GUEST COMING SOON!

Makes big charts to show the weather,
teaches us to work together.

Computer work is fun, fun, fun!

Teacher shows us how it's done.

TODAY IS
THURSDAY

SPECIAL
GUEST
COMING
SOON!

At music time, she sings a song.
Helps us share, tell right from wrong.

TODAY iS THURSDAY

SPECIAL GUEST COMING SOON!

She fixes us a cozy nook,
reads us an exciting book.

Today we have our special guest—
a treat because we did our best!

TODAY iS
FRiDAY

SPECiAL
GUEST
TODAY!

School week's done. We'll be back Monda
for another learn-and-fun day!